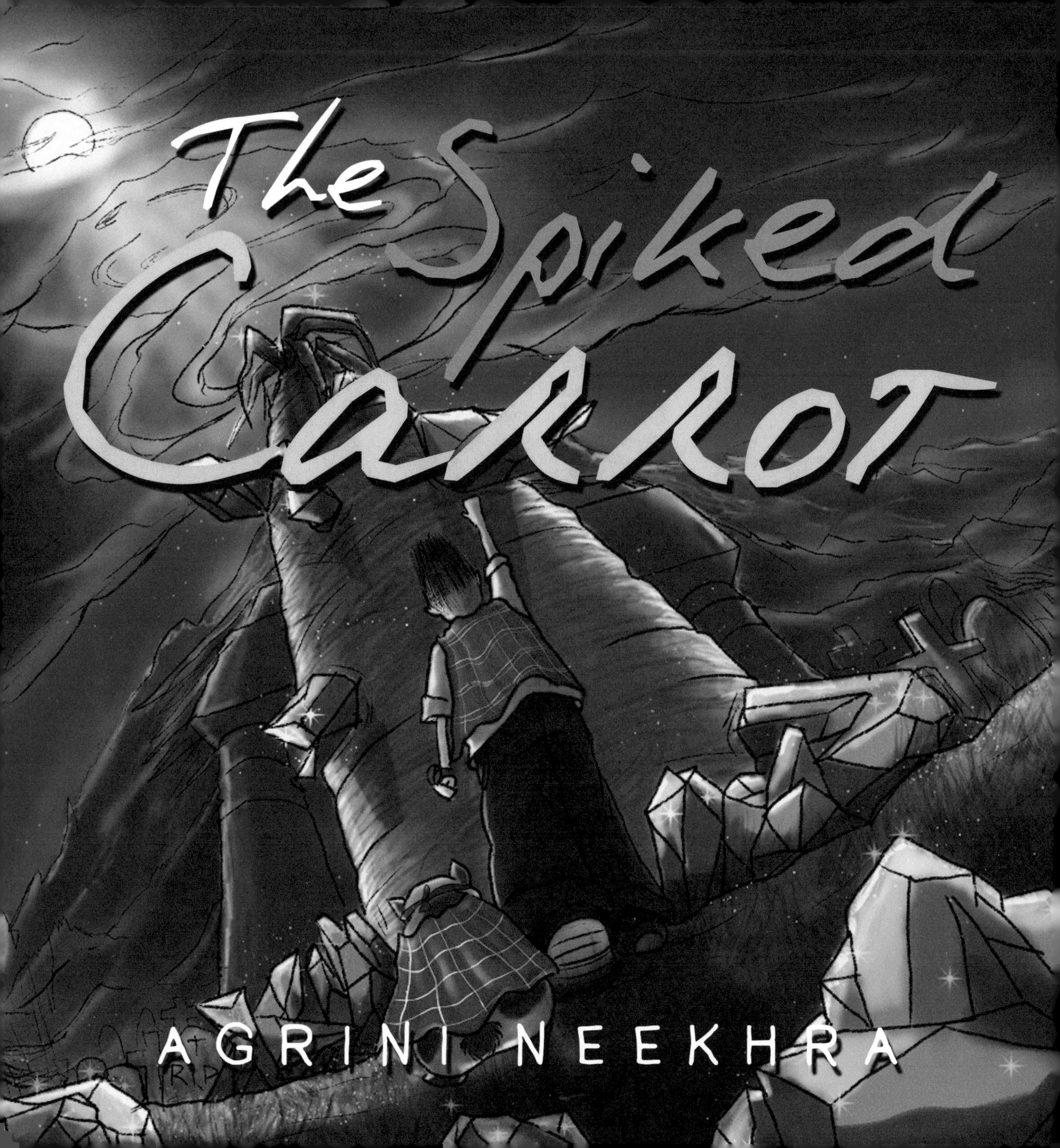
The Spiked Carrot
AGRINI NEEKHRA
RIP

AuthorHouse™
1663 Liberty Drive
Bloomington, IN 47403
www.authorhouse.com
Phone: 833-262-8899

Because of the dynamic nature of the Internet, any web addresses or links contained in this book may have changed since publication and may no longer be valid. The views expressed in this work are solely those of the author and do not necessarily reflect the views of the publisher, and the publisher hereby disclaims any responsibility for them.

Illlustrator: Siddhant Shukla

This book is printed on acid-free paper.

ISBN: 978-1-6655-6091-7 (sc)
ISBN: 978-1-6655-6090-0 (e)

Library of Congress Control Number: 2022910255

Print information available on the last page.

Published by AuthorHouse  07/20/2022

**author**HOUSE®

# The Spiked Carrot

Agrini Neekhra

# Contents

# Prologue

The legendary spiked carrot lay there in the cold, hard ground. Two people cloaked in grey and black hid in the shadows.

"We have to leave it here and bury it," the first person who seemed to be the leader said.

"I understand, but what if he finds it or the magic orb. What about the Books of Everything? It is better to keep the carrot, orb, and Books of Everything with us. It will be safer," the second person said.

"You have a good point, but our forces have weakened very much. He has already used much of our elixir. He has made the elixir medallion. We must destroy it. We will put the flamingo enchantment spell on the orb and Books of Everything," the first person said.

"Okay, let us leave now, before somebody sees us," the second person said.

The first person, who had spoken, then knelt down, and put his hand over the carrot and murmured a few words to the carrot. Then they both hurriedly went away, in the ghastly dark night, but little did they know that somebody was watching from the bushes.

# Chapter 1

## The [Super] Intro

"So everybody, please take out your homework assignments. They should be on pages 35–40. We are talking about pronouns and adv..."

Cut. Sorry for that boring stuff. My pet hamster, who is recording this story is really, really bad. But, he is a hamster, so you have to cut him some slack. Anyways, that woman that you just heard is Mrs. Granger. She loves words. Once there was this boy named Nick Allen and he invented this word "frindle" (for pen), but Mrs. Granger got really angry and she started keeping him after school a lot, but apparently when he was about 30 somethin' he found out that she was rooting for frindle the whole time, which makes no sense to me.

"No, that is not correct. Emily, please tell us the *correct* pronoun. Emily, begi..."

Stop that, I told you to stop. See, I told you he's really bad. Isn't he?..... Hello, hello. Are you there or are you so bored that you're sleeping? And, don't even think about lying to me, because I can hear you snoring from all the way across the paper. Okay, okay I might be boring you to death a little bit. Okay, a lot! So let's get to the story. First,–

Bitty's looking at me like I'm a ghost. Then he points to his index cards.

Oh. I see. I forgot. I'm sorry.

See, Bitty can't talk, but he can write, like really well. Oh, who is Bitty and who is this weirdo who is talking to you, are you asking that? Well if you are, let me just say that I have really great manners. Not. I completely forgot to introduce me and Bitty. Sorry, bad grammar. Bitty and I.

Hi, my name is Einstein Dreamer. I am 10 years old and I live in Sydney, Australia. I am in 5th grade and I go to Outback Primary School.

I like to call myself "Einstein the Superhero" because I am one. I am super, righteous, a risk—taker, nice, good, I never give up, and am very good at science. My teachers call me the Rocket Science Einstein. I always carry my super strength gumballs, which gives me super strength. Did I forget that I am also responsible? My war cry is "To the Rescue!" Pretty vague, but whatever. Now, who is Bitty? Bitty is my pet hamster.

I like to call him the 2nd Superhero or Einstein the Super's Companion. Okay, maybe I put a little too much *me* in there. But, anyways he is very good at handiwork, incredibly small, adorable, cute, very ferocious when angry, very sharp biter, super, good, nice, immune to poison, easily tempted with carrots, and always hungry. Suprisingly, he is only 3 years under me. I am 10, so I think, okay, let's see, ummm......,oh 7. He's 7. But, the most funniest thing is that his war cry is "sniff,sniff, I want a treat." Now, you've learned about the superheroes, it is time to go to the evil villains. Suspense.

# Chapter 2

## The [whatever the opposite of super is] Villains

So, the villains. Hmmm…. Where should I start in their long list of crimes?.......
Anyways, this is Dr. Frazzy.

Boom! Pretty evil, right. See, he even says that he is evil on his shoes. This
is Max.

Looks cute, right. Nope. Up close that tail whacks like a kangaroo and those
teeth snap like Bitty when he's mad and starts biting rubber chew toys in
half. Yikes, it's a sight. Geez, Bitty you don't have to give me THAT look. I'm
just telling the truth. Oh, thaaaat. I am so sorry. I didn't even tell you who the
very, very, very, very, very, very, very, very, very, very, ok I'm getting tired
of saying that, infinity very EVIL villains are.

So, Dr. Frazzy, a so called "scientist" is a villain. Yeah, yeah, I know I said
that he's a villain 100 times, but I have to make myself clear. He is a no good,

evil, mad, (because he's a <u>mad</u> scientist, ha, ha, yeah I know, bad joke, okay, I get it Bitty) bad, immortal (sadly), hard, and ambitious person. His war cry is mwa, ha, ha, ha, ha, ha. As expected. At least my war cry has some words in it. By the way if you're asking about that medal that says I on it, it's his immortality medal. Take that off. Screech. The car stops. He's gone. He's, let's see, let's just say that he is a lot of centuries old. Who knows how old? He made it when he was around his 30s. He stole the elixir from the green forces (the keepers of elixir) and then made the medal. It started to work in his late 80s, when he was *supposed to* decease. But, not only that, it kept his youthfulness and strength also. Enough of him. Wait, he also owns the Book of Everything. There used to be 2 in the world, but now there is only 1 and it is with Dr. Frazzy. This means that Dr. Frazzy knows everything, even about how to take over the world (which is his main motive). As soon as he finds out, we are goners. Let's move on to Max, some terrifying, but less terrifying news than that.

Max is a dog. Max is a bad dog. Max is a very bad dog. Max is an evil dog. So, what I conveyed to you in kindergarten sentences, I hope you understand. What I'm trying to say is that Max is a no good, dirty, evil, ambitious, cunning, ferocious biting, and never leaving Dr. Frazzy's side dog. He is a villain. He is Dr. Frazzy's companion and accomplice. He is the 2nd villain. The good thing about him is that he isn't immortal. It's not like I want him to go bye—bye, but he has been a nuisance lately. Bad news is that he has an unlimited supply of poisonous spikes. Nobody knows why or how. Enough with the introductions, let's get to the story. By the way Max's war cry is "woof, woof," as expected (at least by me).

# Chapter 3

## Sum It Up

To sum it up, my name is Einstein and this here is my companion Bitty. I am 10 years old and Bitty is 7 years old. I am known for my amazing rocket science. But, we both like to call ourselves SUPERHEROES! We have both been tracking down Dr. Frazzy and his evil accomplice, Max for the past two years, when he sadly and unfortunately declared his plan to take over the world. It's up to us to save the world! Let's go!

# Chapter 4

## The Book of Everything

Hey, Bitty, break's over. Time to get back to recording.

"Watson, what is the difference between syno..."

No, ugh, I'm about ready to fire you! Now get on with the *right* recording. Okay, sorry for yelling, just do it correctly.

Bitty and I first put on our secret costumes.

Okay, now, where should I start? Okay, let's see. Ah, yes. We were in our research lab. One month ago.

"Bitty, I have just gotten signals of villain activeness. Can you zoom in and see who exactly it is?" I said.

"It is Dr. Frazzy and Max. They seem to be at their Book of Everything Hideout. I think we should get in our getups and go after them. It has been a long time, since I have pantsed Dr. Frazzy," wrote Bitty.

"Sure, let's go," I said.

We got in our getups and followed the electric signals. (One year ago, we managed to put some kind of chemical in Max's spikes, which will connect to our research lab and our superhero watches. It'll tell us where Max is, and since Max is always with Dr. Frazzy, we will know where he is, too. I'm a genius, aren't I? It was all my idea, and a little of Bitty's)

"Max, come here please. Will you give me the Book of Everything, son?" asked Dr. Frazzy.

"Why isn't he that kind to us, too?" wrote Bitty.

"'Cause we're enemies," I said.

"Ah, let's see, I just have a feeling we'll find it tod...," said Dr. Frazzy.

"Well, well, what is it? The Spiked Carrot. Hmm...Let's read," said Dr. Frazzy.

"The spiked carrot is a magical object, which can be used to gain tremendous amounts of power. To do this, go to the ghastly farms and retrieve it, go to the center of the Earth, the Andes Mountains, and put it in the core corset of the Earth, eat the carrot after it has been thoroughly burnt (fires will appear, once put in corset), and then wish for whatever you desire. The carrot is thought to be by the east side of the ghastly farms where the bushes grow. The green forces, legend has it, put it there," said the Book of Everything.

"Stupid, green forces. Thought they could hide it from me," said Dr. Frazzy.

"Mwa, ha, ha, ha, ha, ha, Mwa ha, ha, ha, ha, ha," cackled Dr. Frazzy.

Meanwhile, Bitty and I were sweating in panic.

"The green forces, that is really bad," I said.

The green forces are people who were the keepers of elixir. They did stuff that was *not* related to elixir, only if it was in a catastrophe crisis. So, if they were trying to hide it from Dr. Frazzy the situation must've been really, really bad.

"Max, pack some cobra venom, weapons, food, water, shovels, dirt, a pot, and extra clothes. NOW!" said Dr. Frazzy.

When, they were done, they got into their special getups.

"Okay, Max. Let's go. We have a world to take over," said Dr. Frazzy.

"Woof, woof," barked Max.

Then, out of nowhere, came, "Not so fast, Dr. Frazzy."

# Chapter 5

## The Police

So, when Bitty and I were following the electric signals, the police also spotted us.

"Officer Hally and Officer Williams, go to the hideout Headquarters and the hideout Book of Everything, of Dr. Frazzy and Max. Check and see if they are there. Report back, if you find anything," said the Chief Officer, Valencia Veronica.

"Yes, ma'am," said Officers Hally and Williams in unison.

"Go!!" yelled the Chief Officer.

They headed to headquarters first, but the villains weren't there, so they went to the Book of Everything hideout. That was when they spotted me.

"Officer Hally, who is that kid?" asked Officer Williams.

"Dunno, but he looks very familiar. (I am good friends with the police.) He looks like—, but he looks like he's heading towards Dr. Frazzy's hideout.

And, why is he wearing that odd outfit and walking in such a weird way?" asked Officer Hally.

"I think we should send a message to the Chief Officer," said Officer Williams.

They sent her a message and then 5 minutes later; they received a message that said, "I'm coming. Wait there."

# Chapter 6

## Spikes, Yikes

"You rascals!" said Dr. Frazzy.

"GO, CHARGE!" I screamed at Bitty.

Bitty went right for Dr. Frazzy's pants and pantsed him. I went for Max's spikes, so I could put some more of the electric chemical water in them. I could put in 27mL on my first try, but I needed to put 5mL more for the chemical to have any effect on him. On my second try, I threw the whole bottle at his spikes, but some of it got in his eyes, so he got really mad at me and shot a bunch of spikes at me and trapped me in a cage. Meanwhile, Bitty was biting and scratching Dr. Frazzy's head and he had already bit Dr. Frazzy's pants off and torn them to pieces. Dr. Frazzy headed for the cobra venom, but I used my super hero cape to knock the bottle off the table. (It can mold into any rope or lasso.) Then, Max shot some more spikes at me. One plunged into my leg. I collapsed onto the floor. There is no cure for this, except if you have someone who can take it out. If you touch it, then it will burn your arm off. Now, if you remember that Bitty is immune to poison, good job! Back to the story. At that time, currently 2 minutes were remaining if my life was to be saved. Luckily, Bitty saw the whole thing and raced to my cage. But, that devil Max blocked Bitty's way, so Bitty bit his foot. Max collapsed and howled. Bitty sniffed the bars and then went through the cage. He started to dig the spike out of my leg and finished just as the 2 minutes ended. Meanwhile, Dr. Frazzy and Max had already headed to the ghastly farms, while we apparently were still stuck in a poisonous, spiked cage. Bitty started to push the spikes out to form a way for our exit, while I started to try and find where Max and Dr. Frazzy were. I had succeeded in trying to put the electric chemical into Max's spikes. When Bitty was finally done, I had found out where Dr. Frazzy and Max were. They were on the east side of the ghastly farms.

"To the Rescue!" I said.

"Sniff, sniff, I want a treat!" sniffed Bitty.

"Let's Go!" I said.

And we headed to the ghastly farms, the first step to save the world.

# Chapter 7

## The Misunderstanding

In 10 minutes, the Chief Officer arrived at Crime Ave where I was spy walking.(You might be wondering how I was spy walking on the same street for 15 minutes. Well, I was spy walking really slowly.)

"So, is this the kid, Officers?" asked the Chief Officer.

"Yes, Ma'am," said Officer Hally.

"Williams?" asked the Chief Officer.

"Yes, Ma'am," said Officer Williams.

"Why is he walking like that? Why is he wearing that strange suit? And most important, why is he heading towards Dr. Frazzy's hideout?" asked Officer Hally.

"You fools. Wasting my time. Don't know a thing about being an officer. Don't you understand? He's walking like that, because he's spy walking and he's wearing a green secret agent suit, which means to your "most important" question, he is a secret agent of Dr. Frazzy," exclaimed the Chief Officer.

"Then, why does he have a pet with him?" ventured Officer Williams.

"Fool, Dr. Frazzy has a pet dog. Why can't that person have a pet guine—no, hamster, WHY CAN'T THAT PERSON HAVE A PET HAMSTER, YA STUPID FOOLS!" yelled the Chief Officer.

"We are both very sorry for wasting your time and questioning you, Chief Officer," said Officer Hally.

"Ya should be fellas. Now, what do you think you're doin' standin' around for nothin'? Huh? Go after him. NOW!" said the Chief Officer.

As they started to go, the Chief Officer stopped them.

"Stop, I'm coming with you both. I'm convinced that you'll both do something wrong," said the Chief Officer.

And, they followed us and found some, let's just say, some, news. Yeah, that suits, whatever's going to happen, well.

# Chapter 8

## The ghastly farm and Flamencia

When we got to the east side of the ghastly farm, we saw Dr. Frazzy and Max digging furiously. It was 3:47 pm exact at that time. At 5:00 p.m. all the ghosts and spirits would come out and terrorize all the human beings and kind of make them go "bye bye". Heh–Heh. So, I was kind of scared. Dr. Frazzy didn't notice us, so we got down to digging, Bitty and I dug for one whole hour. At 4:47 pm, I started to get a little frantic. Dr. Frazzy seemed to be desperate. I wondered if he knew about the 5:00 pm deadline. I noticed that he had changed his pants. They weren't ripped now. That's when I saw it. The Spiked Carrot! It was about 20 yards from me, but it was 10 yards from Dr. Frazzy. It was perpendicular to the sun, which was shining above us.

"Look Bitty, the Carrot," I said.

Bitty looked up at the carrot and then me. Unfortunately, Dr. Frazzy looked up at me and snarled, and then looked at the carrot. It was long and slender and green and it had evergreen spiked gems all over it. The top of it was an elegant checkered light and dark gold. Bitty and I ran for it and Max and Dr. Frazzy also ran for it, but unfortunately they got there first. They got the carrot.

"Dr. Frazzy, change your ways, please let people live happily. Just put the carrot down and walk away. You can be a good man. Just change your ways. Please," I said.

That's all I had left to say to him.

"Well, I'm not going to. Let's go, Max," said Frazzy.

And he threw a jar at Bitty. I soon realized what it was, the sealable jar. The sealable jar is a jar that seals itself around something forever and is not breakable. I was dumbstruck. Where had he gotten it from? Ahh, "The Book of Everything." Now, how would I get Bitty out? I gasped, the super strength gumballs.

I took one out and started chewing it, then I started to pound on the jar, and after I made a small dent, Bitty came out. Evan a small dent or a small crack will make the whole jar crumble. Then I realized that it was 4:59 pm. Dr. Frazzy and Max had already left. I wondered how far it was from Sydney, Australia to Andes Mountains, South America. They would probably go on their private jet, "Evil Wind". I had no idea how I would get to the Andes. I had no money. Maybe, some miracle would happen. Anyways, I reached into my gumball bag to give one to Bitty, so he could also fight the ghosts and spirits, but I found a giant ball instead, in my bag.

"Einstein Dreamer, press the purple button on your superhero watch, please," the ball said.

"Who are you, I mean what are you?" I asked.

"No time for questions, just do it," the ball said.

"Bu–Bu, Bu, Wh–Wha, Wha–," I sputtered.

Just then, a giant tiger faced us. I froze in terror. Bitty pressed the purple button on my watch. It is for giving control of your mind to somebody else. Instantly, I kicked him in the face and he dropped down dead. I put 27 zombies, 23 lions, 17 tigers, 29 mummies, 57 vampires, and 5 animal villains to "bye bye." The rest fled to their respective homes. I felt great. Bitty pressed the pink button on my watch. That's for getting your power back.

"Now, who are you?" I demanded to the ball.

"I guess you deserve to know. I am the keeper of the magic orb, Flamencia Disvardi, pronounced Fla—men—chee—uh. I have come to tell you a story," said the orb.

"Well, right now, I'm in a rush to get to the Andes Mts. So, I guess you'll have to tell me this story some other time, Miss Flamencia Disvardi," I said.

"I know as well as you do that you have no money. I also saved you from those monsters. You could pay me back," said Flamencia.

"Look really, I really thank you for that very much. Thank you, infinity times. But, if I want to save the world, I have to go," I said.

"You can go, after listening to my story. This story will help you on your journey. Tell you what, how about this, you listen to my story first, then I will get you there to the Andes mountains as fast as light. Okay?" said Flamenci,

"OK," I said reluctantly.

She began.

*"Once, when the green forces were prospering, I was a living girl. I had an elder sister, a mother, and father. My mother did fortune telling, my father was an advisor of the mayor of our city, and my sister, she was different from everybody. Everybody talked and was cheerful, she was quiet and read all the time. She wanted to know everything. I liked to fortune—tell and practice magic. One day, my mother went to work. I was going to come with her, but I was very sick, so I stayed home. At work, a man came to my mother.*

*"Will you fortune tell by my hands?" He asked.*

*"I am sorry, sir. I fortune tell only by eyes," she said.*

*My mother was the best fortune teller in the city. Whatever she said, came true.*

*"Okay, then. How much do you charge?" He asked.*

*"Twenty Australian dollars," she replied.*

*"What? Only 20! That little! I offer you fifty Australian dollars," he exclaimed.*

*My mother was quiet for some time. Then she said, "Okay, come along."*

*When they were in the fortune telling chamber, she looked deep into his eyes and turned pale at what she saw. Then, finally she closed her eyes and tried to word what she saw. She could have lied, but she told the truth.*

"Sir, I am very sorry, but I must tell you. You are destined to put a woman to death and hurt her family very deeply," she uttered. She said these words like she truly knew what was about to happen.

"What, what, you daughter of a pig, what," he sputtered. Without thinking, he took a pistol and fired it at her.

After my mother's death, we dwelled in sadness. My father spent more time at political meetings. My sister studied harder at learning everything. I studied harder at learning everything about fortune telling. Then one day, at a political meeting my father spoke against the Mayor. They took him to prison. One month later, my sister went to the bookstore and bought a Book of Everything. It was disguised as a normal book, but she saw what it really was. She got to know the secrets of world. She knew everything. When the green forces' elixir (the nectar of immortality) got stolen by Dr. Frazzy, she knew they were going to hide the spiked carrot at the ghastly farms, so she went to the ghastly farms. She saw where they hid it and what they talked about. They had talked about several things, but one of the things was about the Books of Everything. Notice that it is plural. One of her dreams was to work with the green forces. She thought they meant her, as a book of everything. She knew all the secrets that the normal Book of Everything knew. There could only be two. There was only one book, so the other had to be a person. She was correct, but the green forces didn't know it was her, specifically. So, after they had left she went to the Spiked Carrot and wished she was a book of everything. Since, it was only a transformation, she did not have to go to the Andes Mountains. (If you wish to transform yourself into something else, from the spiked carrot, it will transform you, without you having to go to the Andes.)

The next morning, she had turned into a Book of Everything. When I got up, I saw she wasn't at home, so I thought she was at the bookstore. When I started to study that morning, I saw two Books of Everything. (As you know books of everything are blank, you ask them a question and it appears). I was working on a writing assignment so I took some paper from the less delicate looking book. (I thought my sister had made a copy of the book. For example, if a thief came and asked for the Book of Everything, she would give him the fake book.) By nightfall, I started to worry. My sister still hadn't come back. That's when I remembered about the Book of Everything that I hadn't destroyed. I went to the book and asked it where my sister was.

"Foolish girl, I am your sister," my sister/book said.

She told me the whole story. She told me that now that I had destroyed the other book, the Green forces wouldn't believe her that she was the other human book of everything. They would see only 1 book, so they would think she was the book and not the human book. I told her I would take her to the green forces, the next morning.

She was right! They didn't believe us. I tried to persuade them so much that they got so angry that they turned me into a magic orb and destroyed the one they had before. The other one was dying anyways, so they needed another one. Then they put the Flamingo enchantment spell on us. It is a spell that will send us to the people who need us, but who have also done *at least one good deed. Dr. Frazzy needed my sister to take over the world. He had saved Max's life when Max was homeless. You needed me to save you from the monsters and you are trying to save the world.* That is my story. How does this help you? One act can go a long way. That one man, who killed our mother, made our family dwell in darkness and sadness. He put our father to prison. He became more involved in political activities. That man led my sister to disaster. She studied harder at learning everything. And, he led me to this form, a magic orb. He destroyed my whole family. That statement will help you. Now stand up, hold me, and think about the Andes Mts. Wait, also when the time comes, remember the three life rules," said Flamencia.

And I was off to the Andes Mts.

# Chapter 9

## News

The police reached the hideout, moments after we went to the ghastly farms. (Officer Williams had to take a bathroom break and I guess it took, quite a long time. I don't think the Chief Officer was too happy about that.)

"So, they aren't here," said the Chief Officer, looking right at Officer Williams. (because of the bathroom incident)

Officer Williams just bowed his head and lowered his gaze, feeling ashamed.

"Let's ask the Book of Everything," said Officer Hally said. Dr. Frazzy had left it on the table, because he was in a hurry.

"Go, ahead," said the Chief Officer.

Officer Hally asked where we were.

"Dr. Frazzy, Max, and the people that you call Dr. Frazzy's accomplices who are actually Einstein and Bitty, are at the Andes Mountains," said the Book of Everything.

The book told them what the spiked carrot was, what had happened, and where the villains and we, the superheroes would surface— Cancun, Mexico.

"Oh, no, we have to get Dr. Frazzy and Max to the lock—up. We have to make sure Einstein and Bitty are safe. I hope they're not hurt," said Officer Williams, feeling better, because the Chief Officer's inference of us, Einstein and Bitty, being Dr. Frazzy's partners, was wrong.

Meanwhile, Officer Hally, also had a very high spirit, because of the Chief Officer's wrong inference. The Chief Officer had lowered her gaze in shame and was silent.

"No worries, mate, she'll be right! For right now, let's go!" said Officer Hally.

Officers Hally and Williams ran out of the hideout, leaving the embarrassed Chief Officer behind. Knowing she had no choice, but to follow them, she went out of the hideout, following behind the 2 officers, silently.

# Chapter 10

# The Serpents and the Spiked Carrot

"Come on Bitty, we have to get to the center of the Earth, fast," I said.

We had reached the Andes Mountains. I saw that, right by the entrance of the Andes Mountain, was the Evil Wind Jet parked. We went inside and saw some stairs that said "Center of the Earth, Beware." I wondered why the sign said "Beware." (I later found out, that there were lots of tunnels that fell vertically, to unknown and dark regions. If you fell into one, then who knows what would happen to you.) We headed for the stairs when 3 ginormous serpents confronted us and blocked our way. The 1st was blue, the 2nd was scarlet, and the 3rd was brown, who seemed to be the leader.

"Howdy, ready to be drowned alive? I'm the water serpent," said the blue, water serpent, slyly.

"Hello there, ready to be burnt, alive? I'm the fire serpent," said the scarlet, fire serpent, evilly.

"G'day, ready to be crushed alive? I'm the earth serpent," said the brown, earth serpent, terrifyingly.

"Hello," I said, timidly.

I thought how I would defeat them. Just, then the water serpent lunged at me and made a circular wave of water all around Bitty and I, ready to drown us, when suddenly I had it, the 3 life rules— "Water kills fire. Earth kills water. Pollution kills Earth. Then, I remembered Flamencia's words, "one act can go a long way." A plan formed in my mind. If I used the water serpent to kill the fire serpent, the earth serpent would hopefully get angry and kill the water serpent. Then, maybe I could find some litter and throw it at the earth serpent. Now, I just had to put the plan to action. I used my super cape to whip the water serpent towards the fire serpent. The water serpent lost control of his body and landed on the fire serpent. The fire serpent dropped on the ground and burnt to ashes. As expected, the earth monster got really, really angry. I guess the fire and earth serpents were best friends.

"What have you done? You have killed the fire serpent!" yelled the earth serpent.

"I did not mean to. I promise. That— that boy made me do it. We must make him pay," said the water serpent.

"I do not care. That boy will pay, but you will pay too!" screamed the earth serpent.

And with that, he pounced onto the water serpent. The water serpent splashed onto the ground and made a puddle of blue water mixed with soil, sand, and dirt. Then, I looked around and saw lots of tin cans, empty water bottles, and dirty napkins littered on the ground. Most of the litter had labels that said "Property of Dr. Frazzy" or "Property of Max." Ridiculous. But, it must have kept the serpents away. Serpents don't like human food. So, Bitty and I gathered all the litter we could get and held it. The earth serpent had turned his back to us. He looked at both of the remains of the serpents and then turned around and snarled. We hurled all the litter we had at him. He had faded into a mountain of soil, dirt, sand, and mud. I stood there for a few moments and then Bitty and I ran down the stairs.

We reached there, just as Dr. Frazzy was about to put it in the core set. I pushed Dr. Frazzy. He pushed me back. I lost control of my body and fell into a tunnel, which happened to be the way to the darkest part of the Earth. Bitty, meanwhile was biting and scaffolding with Max. He heard me crying out for help. As I said, Bitty is very good at handicraft, so he vomited all the food in his stomach, which kept Dr. Frazzy and Max a distance away, and started to form the food into a rope. He threw it down to me. I grabbed it and pulled myself up. (It was pretty gross, but I wanted to save my life, so I did it.) By the way, Dr. Frazzy was putting ice cubes in his mouth, to make sure he didn't burn his mouth when he ate the burnt carrot, while I was pulling myself up. When he was done, just as the carrot was about to touch the core set Bitty and I came to our senses. (We were reuniting with each other.) Bitty came to his senses a second, before I did. Bitty jumped up and since he was really, really hungry, he ate the spiked carrot. Because, after all it was a carrot, which was his favorite food. (By the way, no powers came to him, because the carrot wasn't put in the corset, it hadn't burnt thoroughly, and he hadn't wished for anything, either.)

# Chapter 11

## Cancun

"We have to tell Einstein's parents," said Officer Hally.

"Yes, we should," said Officer Williams.

"Let's go and fast," said the Chief Officer, coming to her senses.

They went to my parents and told them everything that had happened. They also contacted the Cancun police. Then, they all headed to Cancun, Mexico, where the villains and us, the superheroes would hopefully surface.

# Chapter 12

## The Elevator

"You scoundrels. You rascals. You destroyed the carrot. Now, I will never take control of the world again!" cried Dr. Frazzy.

Bitty and I saw our chance, so we pushed Max and Dr. Frazzy into the "EXIT" marked elevator and then we hopped in. When, the doors opened we were shocked.

# Chapter 13

## The Victory

There was a huge crowd outside. The Cancun police were at the front of the crowd. The police immediately put Dr. Frazzy in handcuffs and Max on a metal, steel chain and led them to a police car. A day later, I was reunited with my parents, who had reached Cancun, by then. My parents hugged me and embraced me and were like, "What would've happened to us if something happened to you." It was crazy. People kept asking me for my autograph and for Bitty's paw print. Then, the chief police officer, Valencia Veronica came back and congratulated Bitty and I for our heroic deeds and kept thanking us for keeping Australia and the whole world safe. I told them that that's what we're here for. Then the press came. I was modest and told them that it wasn't me that saved the day, it was Bitty. I told them how he cured my poisonous leg, saved me from falling into a tunnel forever, and also how he destroyed the spiked carrot. Not to mention, he also kept me company. The next day, I met with the Prime Minister, Malcolm Turnbull. Bitty and I also received the Australia Medal, the highest award a citizen can receive. Bitty and I both had a lot of fun.

# Chapter 14

## Einstein Dreamer

So, we did trap the evil Dr. Frazzy and his accomplice Max, and now we are goi—

"Einstein, Einstein, Einstein Dreamer, do you hear me? This is not napping class, this is ELA class. You are not to be day dreaming in class. What secret does Matilda get to know after Chapter 9? Do you know the answer?....... No, you do not. You do not know the answer. No wonder your name is Einstein *Dreamer*!!"

# Agrini Neekhra

Agrini Neekhra is the author of the, "Spiked Carrot." She lives in Peoria, Illinois. Agrini was 10 when she wrote this book. She did have a pet hamster named Bitty, pronounced Bit-tee, who is sadly now deceased. He was very active and many of his characteristics are described in this book.

Printed in the United States
by Baker & Taylor Publisher Services